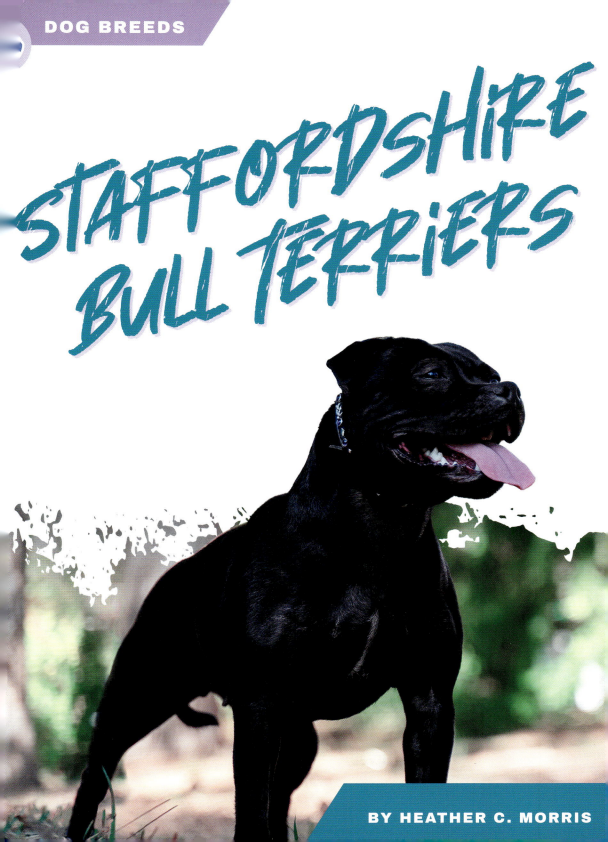

DOG BREEDS

STAFFORDSHIRE BULL TERRIERS

BY HEATHER C. MORRIS

WWW.APEXEDITIONS.COM

Copyright © 2025 by Apex Editions, Mendota Heights, MN 55120. All rights reserved. No part of this book may be reproduced or utilized in any form or by any means without written permission from the publisher.

Apex is distributed by North Star Editions:
sales@northstareditions.com | 888-417-0195

Produced for Apex by Red Line Editorial.

Photographs ©: Shutterstock Images, cover, 1, 4–5, 6, 7, 8–9, 10–11, 12, 14, 16–17, 18, 20, 21, 22–23, 24–25, 26, 27; iStockphoto, 13, 19, 29

Library of Congress Control Number: 2023922100

ISBN
978-1-63738-914-0 (hardcover)
978-1-63738-954-6 (paperback)
979-8-89250-051-7 (ebook pdf)
979-8-89250-012-8 (hosted ebook)

Printed in the United States of America
Mankato, MN
082024

NOTE TO PARENTS AND EDUCATORS

Apex books are designed to build literacy skills in striving readers. Exciting, high-interest content attracts and holds readers' attention. The text is carefully leveled to allow students to achieve success quickly. Additional features, such as bolded glossary words for difficult terms, help build comprehension.

TABLE OF CONTENTS

CHAPTER 1
STRENGTH AND SPEED 4

CHAPTER 2
STAFFY HISTORY 10

CHAPTER 3
STAFFY SPECIFICS 16

CHAPTER 4
CARE AND TRAINING 22

COMPREHENSION QUESTIONS • 28
GLOSSARY • 30
TO LEARN MORE • 31
ABOUT THE AUTHOR • 31
INDEX • 32

CHAPTER 1

STRENGTH AND SPEED

A Staffordshire bull terrier crouches low. When her owner gives the signal, the dog jumps. She bites a toy hanging from a tall wall. For a moment, she **dangles** in the air.

Staffordshire bull terriers can jump up to 6 feet (1.8 m) off the ground.

In the broad jump, dogs must not knock down any of the poles or boards.

The dog is at a **competition**. Her second event is the broad jump. Rows of poles lie on the ground. The dog leaps over them.

STAFFORDTIMES

StaffordTimes is a competition held in the Netherlands. Dogs compete in five events. They leap over **obstacles** and climb high walls. The dog with the most points wins.

Staffordshire bull terriers compete in many types of dog sports.

The **A-frame** is next. The dog races up and down its steep sides. She shows her speed and **agility**.

FAST FACT

Some events test dogs' agility by having them run through obstacle courses.

Weave poles are common obstacles at agility courses. Dogs curve in and out between them.

CHAPTER 2

Staffy History

The Staffordshire bull terrier comes from England. In the 1700s, people wanted powerful dogs to use in dogfights. They mixed sturdy bulldogs with quick terriers.

Today, dogfights are banned in most places. But Staffordshire bull terriers are still brave and tough.

Many bull and terrier dogs were bred to work on farms, not fight.

By the 1800s, these dogs were called "bull and terriers." One type became popular with coal miners living in Staffordshire. People called the dogs Staffordshire bull terriers, or Staffies.

PIT BULLS

Several other dog **breeds** come from the bull and terrier mix. They include the American Staffordshire terrier and the bull terrier. These breeds and Staffies are sometimes called pit bulls.

The term *pit bull* is used for several dog breeds. All have short fur and blocky heads.

In the late 1800s, Staffies spread to other countries. Many places banned dogfights. So, people bred Staffies to be pets instead.

FAST FACT

Most Staffies are friendly to people and good with children.

Staffies love and protect their owners. They make good watchdogs.

CHAPTER 3

STAFFY SPECIFICS

Staffies are small but strong. They stand only 16 inches (41 cm) tall. But Staffies can weigh between 24 and 38 pounds (11 and 17 kg). Most of their weight comes from muscle.

Even a Staffy's head has strong muscles.

Despite their short legs, Staffies can run fast.

Staffies have wide heads and thick necks. Their chests are broad, and their legs are short.

JAWS OF STEEL

Staffordshire bull terriers have powerful jaws. They were bred to bite hard and hang on during fights. As a result, many Staffies love to chew. However, they rarely bite people.

Owners should give their Staffies plenty of chew toys.

Many Staffies have fur that is black or reddish brown.

Staffies have short, smooth fur. They come in many colors. Their fur often has patches of white.

Some Staffies have blue-gray fur.

FAST FACT
The actor Tom Holland has a Staffy named Tessa.

CHAPTER 4

CARE AND TRAINING

Staffies' short fur only needs weekly brushing. But Staffies need exercise every day. They are an energetic breed.

Staffies should exercise for at least one hour each day.

Staffies also need lots of attention. If left alone, they may dig or chew. Owners should spend time playing with and training their Staffies.

FAST FACT

Many Staffies love to run and hike with their owners.

Owners can train their dogs to fetch Frisbees or do other tricks.

With the right training, Staffy puppies can grow up to be friendly.

Staffies are **loyal** and smart. They want to please people. But some may be **aggressive** to other dogs. As a result, this breed is best for **experienced** owners.

EARLY TRAINING

Staffies may be cautious around other dogs. But training can help. Owners can bring their puppies many places. They can have puppies meet many people and dogs. This helps puppies learn to stay calm.

Using leashes on walks can help Staffies stay safe around other dogs.

COMPREHENSION
QUESTIONS

Write your answers on a separate piece of paper.

1. Write a few sentences about the history of the Staffordshire bull terrier.

2. Would you want to own a Staffy? Why or why not?

3. Where does most of a Staffy's weight come from?

    A. muscle

    B. bones

    C. fat

4. Why might bringing a dog many places help it learn to stay calm?

    A. The dog can learn to be alone.

    B. The dog can try new foods.

    C. The dog can get used to new sights and sounds.

5. What does **crouches** mean in this book?

A Staffordshire bull terrier **crouches** *low. When her owner gives the signal, the dog jumps.*

   A. eats

   B. bends down

   C. barks

6. What does **energetic** mean in this book?

But Staffies need exercise every day. They are an **energetic** *breed.*

   A. active

   B. noisy

   C. lazy

Answer key on page 32.

GLOSSARY

A-frame
Two ramps leaned together to form a point at the top.

aggressive
Strong and quick to attack.

agility
Being able to move quickly and easily.

breeds
Specific types of dogs that have their own looks and abilities.

competition
An event where people or animals try to beat others.

dangles
Hangs above the ground.

experienced
Having skills or knowledge in something as a result of doing it before.

loyal
Loving and staying true to a person or thing.

obstacles
Things that block the way.

TO LEARN MORE

BOOKS

Green, Sara. *Terriers*. Minneapolis: Bellwether Media, 2021.

Higgins, M. G. *Working Dogs*. Newport Beach, CA: Saddleback Educational Publishing, 2020.

Pearson, Marie. *Dog Behavior*. Minneapolis: Abdo Publishing, 2024.

ONLINE RESOURCES

Visit **www.apexeditions.com** to find links and resources related to this title.

ABOUT THE AUTHOR

Heather C. Morris writes books for kids who love science and imagination. She lives in the foothills of the Appalachians with her family, which includes their beloved border collie/Great Pyrenees mix.

INDEX

A
A-frame, 8
aggressive, 26
agility, 8

B
breeds, 13

C
chewing, 19, 24
competition, 6–8

D
dangles, 4

E
England, 10
events, 6–8
exercise, 22

F
fur, 20, 22

L
loyal, 26

O
obstacles, 7–8

S
Staffordshire, England, 12

T
training, 24, 27

ANSWER KEY:
1. Answers will vary; 2. Answers will vary; 3. A; 4. C; 5. B; 6. A